They w̲ ̲ ̲
and st̲ ̲ ̲ ̲ ̲ ̲ ̲ ̲ ̲ ̲ ̲ ̲der a tall
pine. '̲ ̲ ̲ go up, you're the best
climber,' said Tim, holding his hands
joined ready for Gerry's foot and a lift
up.

Within a few seconds Gerry was
high up the bare trunk.

'There's a great white house all
boarded up,' he called in a loud
whisper.

'There's no one in sight, it's all
wild and overgrown. I think it's deserted.'

The Strange House

Written and Illustrated by
Raymond Briggs

Beaver Books

A Beaver Book

Published by Arrow Books Limited
17–21 Conway Street, London W1P 6JD

An imprint of the Hutchinson Publishing Group

London Melbourne Sydney Auckland
Johannesburg and agencies throughout the world

First published by Hamish Hamilton 1961
Beaver edition 1977
Reprinted 1985

Set in Monotype Baskerville

Printed and bound in Great Britain by
Cox & Wyman Ltd, Reading

ISBN 0 09 941860 6

Contents

I

Tadpoles and Golf Balls

Gerry Martin and his friend Tim Rogers were out to look for tadpoles. Despite the sunshine Tim was feeling unhappy about going.

'I don't like the idea,' he said. 'It's not worth getting caught.'

'Oh, it's all right, Tim, we're not going to do any harm,' replied Gerry. 'We're only going just inside the wall where it's all overgrown. They won't mind that because they play golf much farther in.'

Tim and Gerry lived in the suburbs and the only place for catching tadpoles was in the stream which ran through the local golf course. Gerry had been on the golf course before, with older boys, looking for golf balls. More than once he had been seen and chased by roaring red-faced golfers. So he was feeling very brave and superior to Tim who had never once been there. They were soon walking beside the wall which ran round this side of the golf course.

'Here's the place we get over,' said Gerry, 'by the hawthorn bush, the stream comes out just underneath it. Mind your head on the wire.'

The two boys climbed over the wall then rolled down the steep bank in the thick tussocks of grass.

'Here's the stream,' said Gerry. 'See it comes out of that pipe from under the road. It's not very deep – look, somebody's paper boat has just come through the pipe.'

But Tim was crouching in the grass like a frightened sentry in the jungle, not listening at all.

'I can't see any golfers, yet,' he whispered.

'There aren't many today, it's on Sundays you get a lot,' said Gerry, talking even louder than necessary just to show off. 'Come down into the stream here, then they won't see you.'

The stream ran between steep banks and when Gerry crouched down on a stone only his head showed above the grass.

Tim did not hesitate and quickly wriggled

through the grass keeping as low down as possible. He was so anxious to take cover that when he reached the edge he fell forwards into the stream up to his elbows.

'Help, Gerry, I'm stuck, I can't get back,' he cried,' his nose almost touching the water.

Gerry was laughing so much at Tim that he practically sat down in the stream himself.

'Hang on Tim, I'm coming.'

He jumped up on to the bank, ran round to Tim, seized his ankles and pulled him up.

'Oh! Thank goodness,' said Tim. 'Another

second and I'd have drowned, my arms ache like anything.'

'Come on, don't lie there groaning all day,' said Gerry pulling out a roll of sacking from under his coat and a big jam jar from each pocket. 'Let's start dragging.'

Tim pushed their lunch bag into the nettles, and they both took off their shoes and socks.

'We'd better tie them round our necks in case we have to run for it,' said Tim.

'Good idea,' Gerry replied as he rolled up his trousers and dropped into the stream. 'Let's try

up at the end where the stream comes in, it's deeper there.'

They dragged the sack through the water, each holding two corners. Every third or fourth time there were several tiny, black tadpoles wriggling in the wet, brown sacking.

After about half an hour Tim said, 'Look, we've got loads already, so let's go before any golfers come.'

'All right,' said Gerry, looking at the wriggling tadpoles in the jars. 'Gosh! Tim. I almost forgot to tell you. You know that queer couple we saw on the bus that day? The old woman you said was like a witch and the little girl like a fairy?'

Tim nodded.

'Well, I think I saw them again. You know I came home after midnight on Friday, with my father in the car? Well, we were coming down Church Road when we saw a little girl in a

nightdress running down the road and being chased by an old woman all in black.'

'Golly!' said Tim. 'What happened?'

'Dad stopped the car and he was going to get out, but the old witch caught up with the girl and they walked back together, so we drove on. Dad said no one was doing anything wrong, so we couldn't interfere. The little girl was crying, though.'

'She was crying in the bus too,' said Tim. 'It seems as if she's always crying. I bet that old girl is a witch, just like I said.'

'Look, there's another pink boat,' said Gerry. He picked it up as it ran against their sack and tossed it on to the bank. 'I know, let's try and get a frog too. He could live in your garden.'

'Well, all right,' said Tim, 'but we ought to go soon, and —'

PLOP!

'I bet that's one, that splash!' cried Gerry excitedly. 'It was up there. Look! You can see the rings. Come on!' Gerry waded up the stream as fast as he could go with Tim close behind. Suddenly he stopped.

'Oh golly! It's not a frog at all, it's a golf ball!' cried Gerry, staring wide-eyed at the little white ball sitting smugly on the stream bed. 'We've had it now, they'll be here in a minute, they must have seen it come in here!'

Even as Gerry spoke they heard voices coming nearer.

'It's them! It's them!' squeaked Tim, crouching lower.

'Over there on the left, old man,' boomed a voice. 'I expect it's in the stream.'

'Oh! Oh! They're bound to come now,' whispered Tim. 'We can't get over that wire in time in bare feet!'

'We'll have to make a dash for the far side,' said Gerry, biting his lip. 'They'll never catch us – here goes!'

Gerry leaped up out of the stream and ran furiously away. Tim leaped after him, slipped in the mud and slid back into the stream.

'It's those kids again,' bellowed a voice. 'After 'em!'

'I can't get up! I can't!' whimpered Tim, weak with fright. Then making a last, huge effort he managed to get up on to the bank and sprint after Gerry, his shoes banging painfully up and down on his chest. He could hear the great feet of the golfers pounding after him and he ran faster and faster, his bare feet flying over the springy turf.

From the corner of his eye he saw the red blur of another golfer running up to cut him off. He swerved to the left as the man came lunging up to him, then found he was running straight towards the stream again, which was much wider at this point. He could hear the golfer's breathing behind him and ran even faster. The stream came rushing up – a great stretch of sky-filled water. Tim jumped as he had never jumped before, his shoes jerked up and hit him under the chin – then he landed heavily on the other side. One foot skidded in the mud and splashed into the water, then he was up and away.

The golfer said something furiously to himself then turned and ran back upstream to the plank bridge.

Tim was well ahead now, and by the time the

golfers had galloped over the bridge he could no longer hear the thudding of their feet.

Gerry was disappearing round the curve of a steep slope, and Tim ran harder to catch up with him. He ran round the curve in the hill, hesitated then stopped – Gerry had vanished! The empty golf course stretched far away into the distant wall.

'Get out you little devil!' roared a voice. 'Get on with you.'

The two golfers in red woolly pullovers were puffing up the slope towards him waving their golf clubs like Indians on the war-path.

Tim ran on towards the wall and as he passed a thick thorn tree a voice hissed:

'Tim, here!'

Tim turned and saw Gerry's head sticking out of the thick grass in the shady hollow under the tree.

'Quick, in here.'

Tim dived head first into the hollow, panting for breath.

'Wriggle right down, it's quite deep underneath,' said Gerry.

They looked at one another with wide, scared eyes, bright in the gloom under the dense bush. Their faces were red and trickles of sweat ran from their temples.

'Ssh! There they are,' whispered Gerry.

The two podgy golfers stood on the skyline

holding their aching sides and peering about the empty golf course.

'They sound like two little kids playing trains,' laughed Tim. 'Puff-puff, puff-puff.' He felt happy and secure now that the golfers had lost sight of them and had given up the chase.

After a little more puffing and club waving the two golfers turned their woolly backs and stumped off.

Gerry and Tim curled up, hugging their knees and laughing.

'I say, old man,' boomed Gerry in his deepest voice, 'over there on the left, old man!'

'Get out you little devil, get out!' cried Tim, and they both collapsed on their backs, helpless with laughter.

Suddenly, in the midst of their laughter, Gerry gave a shout. 'Help! I'm going under – Tim – oh help!'

Tim sat up and saw Gerry sliding head first into the roots of the tree, as if being sucked underground.

'Help!' came another muffled shout. Tim seized Gerry's ankles and pulled, but his own feet slipped and he rolled forward on top of Gerry.

Together they slid into the darkness.

2

Under the Ground

Tim and Gerry tumbled over and over down a bumpy slope, with dry leaves rustling in the darkness around them. They sat up in a tangle of legs, shoelaces and leaves at the bottom.

'What happened?' moaned Tim. 'Where are we?'

'It's a great big hole,' said Gerry. 'I fell in backwards – look, that's where we came through.'

They both looked up to the dim circle of light fringed with grass and darkened by thorn twigs.

'Oh, come on Gerry,' said Tim. 'Let's get out, it's cold and damp and horrible in here.'

'Wait a minute,' said Gerry. 'I've got that pencil torch on me.'

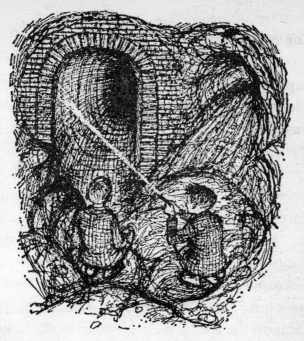

He pulled out the little chromium pencil and pressed the red button at the end. A ray of light cut through the darkness like a sword.

'Gosh, it's super!' cried Tim. 'I've never seen it going in the real dark before.'

They crouched side by side looking along the searching ray as Gerry shone it about the hole.

'Look, Tim,' he cried, 'there's bricks there, it's a wall – a tunnel!'

Tim and Gerry peered as far as possible into the tunnel, but its damp lines of green bricks curved

23

away into darkness.

'Come on, let's explore,' said Gerry, quickly pulling on his shoes and socks.

'Suppose it collapses,' said Tim. 'Those bricks look jolly old and wet. It might cave in and we'd be buried alive for ever.'

'We've just got to chance that, so come on. I'll lead with the torch.'

Gerry was already in the dark tunnel mouth, his torch beam flickering over the green brickwork. Tim did not want to be left alone in the dark so as soon as he had put on his shoes he jumped up and followed close behind Gerry.

'Look out, Tim! there's water. See, it goes into that hole on the left there. We'll have to walk along next to it. It comes all the way down the tunnel.'

The dark passage stretched ahead of them in a green sinuous curve. The stream cackled to itself in the darkness, the air was cold and damp. They plodded slowly forward and Tim sensed the weight of the ground getting heavier and heavier above them as they went deeper under the hill. He felt that the tunnel was a frail hollow which at any moment would be crushed by the tons of earth all about it. The light from the entrance had disappeared and there was nothing but the darkness in front, the darkness behind them and the low, green arch curving close above their heads.

Tim felt a growing terror of being shut in. He longed to run and wave his arms about in freedom. But he shut his eyes tight, and gripped hard on the waist of Gerry's coat until, after what seemed an age, the tunnel widened and became much higher.

'What's that?' cried Tim suddenly, clutching Gerry's coat again. Gerry shone his torch towards the stream where Tim pointed, and there, speeding down the current was a pink paper boat.

'It's another of those pink boats,' said Gerry, 'that's the third one. This must be the same stream that comes out on the golf course – look! there's some steps.'

The torch beam shone on some rusty iron rungs.

'There's an iron lid at the top, too,' said Tim. 'Let's try and get out.'

'No, not yet, let's go to the end first. I must see where it comes out. We can always come back.'

'All right,' replied Tim. 'Lead on, MacDuff. But I hope it's soon or we'll come out in Australia.'

They walked on round a sharp turning and found the tunnel blocked by a new brick wall.

'Well, that settles it,' said Tim. 'Come on, back to the steps.'

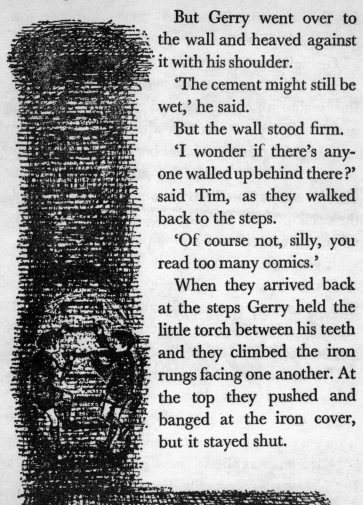

But Gerry went over to the wall and heaved against it with his shoulder.

'The cement might still be wet,' he said.

But the wall stood firm.

'I wonder if there's anyone walled up behind there?' said Tim, as they walked back to the steps.

'Of course not, silly, you read too many comics.'

When they arrived back at the steps Gerry held the little torch between his teeth and they climbed the iron rungs facing one another. At the top they pushed and banged at the iron cover, but it stayed shut.

'Let's both push together at one end,' said Tim, 'that might do it.'

So Gerry moved round and they both stood as close to the lid as possible with muscles braced hard.

'One, two, three – heave!' they chanted together.

With a grinding wrench the lid was flung back. Blinding sunlight and a rush of fresh air swept in on them. The sky was a brilliant blue and the birds were singing.

3
The Strange House

'Gosh! Isn't it lovely?'

Tim jumped out eagerly and rolled over and over in the sunny grass.

'It's so light, and listen to those birds,' he went on.

'Thank goodness we're out of that tunnel,' said Gerry. 'I'd had enough of that.'

'I wonder where we are?' said Tim. 'We'd better watch out, we may be on private property and we'll be prosecuted or something. What is being prosecuted anyway?'

'Same as being executed only worse, I think,' replied Gerry, laughing. 'Keep low, Tim, this grass is long enough to give us cover.'

'Let's crawl to those trees, then we can get up one and see where we are.' Tim began crawling expertly through the grass keeping quite flat to the ground.

They were soon amongst the trees, and stopped together under a tall pine.

'You go up, you're the best climber,' said Tim, holding his hands joined ready for Gerry's foot and a lift up.

Within a few seconds Gerry was high up the bare trunk.

'There's a great white house all boarded up,' he called in a loud whisper. 'There's no one in sight, it's all wild and overgrown. I think it's deserted. Oh, my arms are breaking – look out, Tim – I'm coming down.'

Gerry slackened his grip and slid down the trunk like a fireman down a pole. Chips of bark flew off in his face and a button tore off his coat, then he landed heavily beside Tim.

'Gosh, my hand's bleeding,' he said, looking down at a tiny scratch.

'Serves you right for showing off,' Tim said. 'Shall we explore round the house or find an escape route first?'

'Oh, blow the escape route. The whole place

looks deserted anyway. Come on.' Gerry was already marching off towards the house.

Tim looked about him doubtfully then ran to catch up with Gerry.

Soon they saw the white house, still and silent in the sun. The dark trees behind it hardly stirred.

'Gosh, it looks creepy,' said Tim, 'but it does look deserted, there's grass growing up the front steps. Isn't it big! Just look at those pillars! I bet it was a terrific place once with great coaches, and balls and butlers and things.'

'Let's look all round it,' replied Gerry. 'We may be able to get in and have a look. For all you know there may be a butler there still – a ghost one – all transparent!'

Gerry laughed as Tim stopped dead.

'Golly, yes! It might be haunted,' he cried, gazing wide-eyed at the house.

'I expect that's why it's boarded up,' laughed Gerry, 'to keep the ghosts in.'

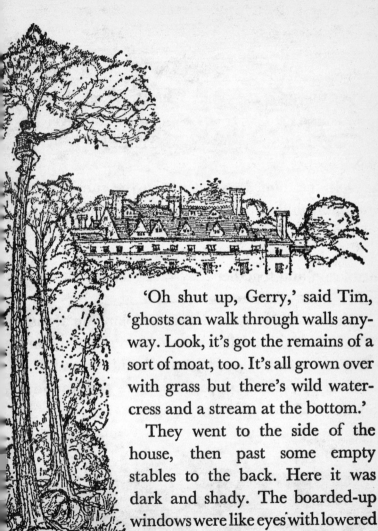

'Oh shut up, Gerry,' said Tim, 'ghosts can walk through walls anyway. Look, it's got the remains of a sort of moat, too. It's all grown over with grass but there's wild watercress and a stream at the bottom.'

They went to the side of the house, then past some empty stables to the back. Here it was dark and shady. The boarded-up windows were like eyes with lowered lids. The upper windows gazed blankly over the trees.

31

'Ooh come on, let's get out in the sun again,' said Tim, pulling Gerry's sleeve. 'It's worse than the tunnel round this side.'

'Yes, it's horrible, let's get away.' Gerry broke into a run and together they raced for the far side of the house and into the sunlight again.

'Oh, that's better,' said Gerry, looking up at the sun. 'I don't think I like this place much. But I'm going in if possible, just to show I'm not scared.'

'Well, yes,' Tim replied, 'but there's no way in, so we can't.'

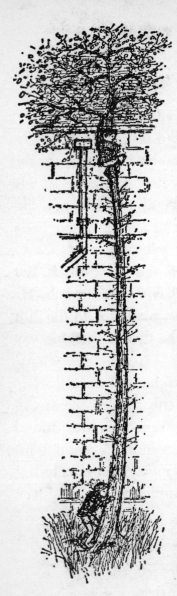

Gerry had stopped and was looking at a solitary tree growing close to the wall of the house.

'I'm not so sure about that. I bet we could get on the roof from that tree.'

'It's a jolly long way up,' said Tim, 'and not many branches.'

'Just you watch, timid Tim,' Gerry replied, running down the bank and jumping the stream.

Gerry twined his arms and legs about the trunk, gripping hard with the edges of his soles. The tree was one of the dusty sort and within seconds his hands and legs were black. Greeny-black powdery stuff covered his shirt and fell tickling down inside. He shut his eyes tight and puffed the dust off his face. He turned to look down and felt a shock at the height he found himself.

Tim seemed just a tiny, white face gazing anxiously upwards.

'Stick it, Gerry,' Tim called.

Gerry's arms felt weak and his legs were beginning to go numb. He looked up and saw that the first branch was still six feet or more away. He clenched his teeth and heaved himself higher. His stomach muscles were shaking and his whole body was beginning to feel weak with panic.

'I can't, I can't,' he whimpered to himself. But at last he was almost level with the branch. He reached out a hand and just managed to touch it with the tips of his fingers; he then inched his way up to get a firm grip.

'Criminals! Criminal burglars! Thieves!'

Gerry was so scared by this sudden screaming voice, he almost let go. He craned his head round and saw a tall, gaunt woman in black, coming towards them. She picked her way awkwardly but swiftly over the rough ground like a huge, black crow.

4
On the Roof

Gerry clung on tightly, not knowing what to do. Suddenly, without having decided anything, he found himself shouting.

'Run for it, Tim, run!'

Tim's worried face looked up at him, then back

at the advancing woman. Again Tim looked up,
poised on his toes, not knowing whether to run or
to climb the tree. But Tim knew the tree was too
much for him, even Gerry had only just managed
it.

Suddenly he was off, running for the trees.

'Criminal vagabond!' cried the woman. She
turned and glared up at Gerry, her fierce eyes and
jutting chin quite frightening even though so far
away.

Gerry quickly looked away, and swung along
the branch to the parapet of the house. He then
lowered himself on to it and dropped down to the
roof.

His thoughts were still in a whirl as he looked at
the bewildering muddle of chimneys and the steep
slopes of gables.

'Shall I try and get back down the tree, or try

and get down through the house?' Gerry thought.

He stood still, biting his lip and almost crying with indecision and fright.

'I wonder if she's still there?'

Gerry lay flat on the parapet and cautiously peered over, half expecting the strange woman to be coming magically up the tree. But she had vanished.

'Oh crumbs! She'll be coming up through the house. I must hide.'

He scrambled up the sloping roof and dropped

down into the angle between a tall chimney stack and the slates. He crouched there trying to think clearly.

'Oh golly, what am I doing? I must be mad sitting here waiting for her to catch me, I must get down.'

Gerry was just about to get to his feet when there was a sharp creak from the other side of the roof. He edged up to the top and peered over. Immediately below him a door had half opened and then stuck. The door shook and the glass in it rattled. It scraped along another inch and Gerry saw a bony hand gripping the knob, the knuckles white with effort.

He turned and slid wildly down the roof. A slate came loose and went clattering down.

'Ah!' came a triumphant shout from the doorway as the door burst open.

Gerry almost dived over the parapet, flinging himself straight at the trunk of the tree, not bothering with the branch. He twined himself about the trunk and slid down. Dust flew in his face and the bark grazed his cheek and knees. Suddenly he stuck.

He looked down and found that a spiky broken branch had gone right through his trousers, scratching his leg. He feverishly pulled the cloth free of the spike. As he regained his hold on the tree, he looked towards the house, and there, staring at

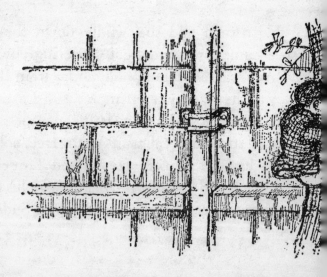

him through the grimy window pane, was a pale, ghostly face.

Gerry started and almost lost his hold.

'Criminal!' came a squawk from above.

Immediately Gerry began sliding swiftly down, careless of being hurt. The woman seized the branch and began madly shaking the tree.

Gerry let go well above the ground, pushed himself clear, and landed skilfully, hardly touching the ground with his hands. Without a pause he was up and running for the safety of the trees.

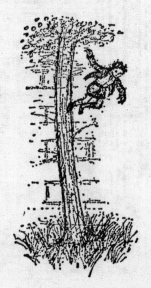

5
Pink Paper Boats

Gerry plunged through the ferns and into the shade and quiet of the trees.

'Gerry! Gerry!' came Tim's voice.

Gerry looked round for Tim but could see no one. Suddenly there was a crash in the bracken just behind him as Tim dropped out of a tree.

'What happened?' Tim asked.

'Never mind now, I'll tell you later, let's get out.'

They ran quickly through the woods until they came to a wall. Although the wall was low on the inside they had to use the ivy to get down the long drop to the pavement.

'Gosh! Look,' said Tim, 'we're in Arthur Road.

I know where we are now. We can easily get back to the golf course from here. I hope the sandwiches are still there, I hid them in the nettles. Now, for goodness' sake, what happened?'

As they walked along Gerry told Tim all that had happened, leaving out the part about nearly crying. Tim listened wide-eyed and secretly envious. 'A face!' he cried when Gerry came to that part of the story. 'It can't be a real one, the whole place is boarded up. I bet it was a ghost!'

'Yes, that's what I thought when I saw it. I almost let go – Tim! of course – that woman! I was so scared I didn't realise. It's the old witch on the bus.'

'Crumbs! Yes,' said Tim, 'it could be, it *was* like her, and the face must be the little girl! But what are they doing in a house that's all shut up?'

'I wonder,' said Gerry, 'it's all jolly odd.'

'Well, I bet she *is* a witch and I bet she's put a spell on that girl.'

'She didn't put much of a spell on me, did she?' grinned Gerry, feeling very brave now that he was safely outside.

'You don't know yet,' said Tim very seriously. 'It may not work for years, or you might suddenly turn into a tadpole tonight and wake up in a jam jar tomorrow morning.' Tim burst into a laugh at his own joke.

'Very funny,' grunted Gerry. But he looked rather less pleased with himself.

'Let's have lunch just inside the wall,' said Gerry when they arrived back at the stream. 'We're well hidden and we can soon get out if somebody comes. There won't be any golfers about at lunch-time anyway.'

'All right,' said Tim, 'it will be better than the pavement.'

They soon lay back in warm sun, eating cheese and chutney sandwiches and guzzling cream soda.

'Oh, what a relief,' sighed Tim. 'We've had a very busy morning, Mr Martin.'

'We have indeed, Mr Rogers,' replied Gerry. 'I wonder just what is going on in that house though?'

'I-wish-I-knew,' said Tim, making big sparkling bubbles rise in the bottle as he gulped cream soda between each word. 'Whatever it is, I'm sure it's something nasty. That old witch is probably boiling up horrible potions and trying them on the girl, and that's why she's always crying.'

'Just a minute,' said Gerry. 'I'll put the tad-poles in the water, they'll die in this heat.'

He leaned down into the stream and lowered the jam jar into the shallow water. A flash of pink caught his eye. He looked up, and there, bobbing away downstream in the sun, was another paper boat.

'Hi, Tim! Another boat has just gone by. That's four we've seen.'

'There must be a factory upstream, making them,' yawned Tim; 'this is probably where they test them out.'

'The old one we threw out is still here,' said Gerry, 'it's all curling up in the sun. Here you are, lazybones.'

Gerry kicked the crumpled boat on to Tim's chest. Tim sat up and pushed it away.

'Oh, let's have some peace, Gerry. I'm too full to move anyway,' he mumbled through a mouthful of fruit cake.

'Now a bit of it has gone inside my shirt.'

He fished it out, and cried, 'Gerry! Look, it's a photograph.'

'Let's see,' said Gerry, leaning over. 'Tim, it's that girl! The one at the house.'

'Gosh, yes. It could be.'

'Have a look at the back,' said Gerry.

Tim turned the photograph over. 'Oh, it's all smudged.'

'There's something at the bottom, though,' said Gerry. 'Move your thumb. Yes, look, it's upside down. Hel—, H, E, L. Perhaps it's her name, Helen.'

'Yes, but what is it doing in the boat,' said Tim. 'Why should anyone sail a paper boat down a stream with someone's photo in it?'

'Tim, that moat thing round the house, could be the same stream as this.'

'Yes,' said Tim, 'it's quite likely.'

'Then she might have sent it herself,' said Gerry.

'Yes; golly! Suppose it means HELP.'

'I bet it does.'

'So do I.'

Gerry jumped to his feet. 'We must get that other boat, there may be a clearer message on that one.'

He ran downstream, through the bushes, and out into the open. He could just see the other boat bobbing along the stream in the distance.

'Hi, you!' came a shout.

'Oh crumbs, not again,' thought Gerry, not stopping to look, but running straight for the boat.

A man appeared far over to his right and started running towards him. Gerry ran on towards the boat. The man came nearer and nearer, but now Gerry could see that the boat had stopped in the middle of the stream. The man was now very near

so Gerry jumped straight into the water, snatched up the boat, and scrambled out on the far side. He ran off with the water squelching in his shoes, his soaked socks clinging to his legs.

'Oh, it's all right,' the man called out. 'I didn't know it was your boat you were after. It's all right.'

'Oh-er, thanks,' faltered Gerry, slowing down and not knowing whether to feel relieved or annoyed.

When he came back he found Tim sitting on the wall, shaking with laughter and singing:

'The daring young man on the flying trapeze,
He flies through the air with the greatest of ease.'

'Oh, shut up,' said Gerry. 'I'm soaked.'

'No, seriously,' said Tim looking very solemn, 'I think you are a very brave little boy. In fact, I think I'll ask my sister to see if she can get you into the Brownies. They're a very tough lot, you know.'

'Will you shut up?' shouted Gerry, then laughed and laughed in spite of himself.

'Come on, let's see the boat,' said Tim when they had recovered.

Gerry carefully pulled the boat apart. 'This one's still quite dry – here it is! It's a different picture of the same girl.'

'Quick, quick, let's see the back.'

Gerry turned the photograph over.

'Help! I am locked up in Park House in Arthur Road. Please, help.'

'Golly,' cried Tim, 'do you think it's real?'

'I wonder,' said Gerry, 'it's a funny sort of joke

if it's not. Besides, it would be a silly waste of photographs.'

'We'd better take it to the police,' said Tim.

'No fear, not yet anyway,' replied Gerry, pulling off his shoes and socks. 'Let's think what to do while these things dry. I vote we try to rescue her ourselves.'

'Sir Lancelot Martin to the rescue,' cried Tim. 'I'll get your horse and armour ready, sire.'

'Will you be serious?' said Gerry, wringing out his socks and draping them on the barbed wire. 'We can always go to the police afterwards if it doesn't come off.'

'Yes, we've got to think,' frowned Tim, as he sat down and bit a gigantic lump out of a huge, green cooking apple.

Gerry sat down facing him and began peeling a large orange.

As their jaws moved steadily they both looked very serious indeed.

6

The High Window

'We'll have to have some sort of plan,' said Tim, as they walked back up the hill to the house. 'We can't do anything while the witch is still there. We'd better lie low and wait for her to come out.'

'Good idea,' said Gerry. 'We could climb a tree and watch for her to leave. We can't just wait outside or she'd see us.'

Suddenly, Tim lunged against Gerry making him fall into the ditch which ran under a laurel hedge beside the pavement.

'What –' cried Gerry.

Tim then flung himself on top of Gerry.

'What are you – ?' gasped Gerry.

'Sh-sh, quiet!' hissed Tim, 'she's coming, on the other side, the witch – she'll be coming past in a minute.'

Tim and Gerry peered through the grass, lying as still as they could in the crackling leaves.

Soon the witch woman came level with them, hardly visible in the deep shade under the beech trees.

'She's got a basket on wheels,' whispered Tim. 'Perhaps that girl's inside it.'

'Oh, rubbish, it's not big enough anyway, not unless she's made her shrink by magic,' said Gerry, with a great grin at Tim.

'Oh, be quiet,' said Tim.

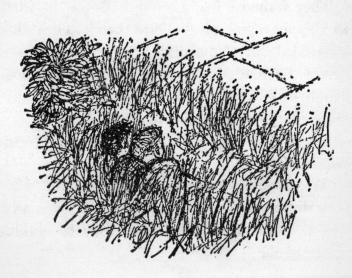

They waited a few more seconds for the witch to disappear round the next bend. Then they scrambled out of the ditch, ran up the hill and across the road to the wall. With a quick look round to make sure no one was watching, they climbed up the ivy and dropped down inside.

'Come on,' said Gerry, 'let's go straight to the window.'

'Why don't we knock first?' said Tim, when they stopped under the window. 'We'd look a bit silly if it was all a joke. There may be nothing wrong at all.'

'Yes, I suppose we'd better,' said Gerry, 'but I bet she doesn't answer. I bet she's locked in.'

They ran round to the front of the house and pressed the bell.

'Can't hear it ring,' said Gerry. 'It looks very old and dead. There's no knocker either.' He knocked hard on the door with his knuckles. A hollow echo sounded inside, but no one came.

'Let's throw gravel up at the window,' said Tim, scooping up a handful from the drive, and running back to the tree. He flung it hard at the high window. It rattled against the glass then showered down on them, making them hunch their shoulders and screw up their faces. Then Gerry threw another handful even harder.

'Careful!' cried Tim, 'you'll crack the glass.'

Suddenly a face appeared at the window.

'It's her!' cried Gerry, waving with both hands.

The girl at the window eagerly waved back. She then tried to open the window. Tim and Gerry watched her trying hard to raise it, but it remained shut fast.

'I'll go and help her,' said Gerry.

He climbed quickly up the tree, reached out for the drainpipe and got one foot on the narrow ledge which ran along to the window-sill. He pushed away from the tree.

'Careful, Gerry,' called Tim, anxiously.

Gerry reached out for the edge of the window and just got his fingers round it. But to move towards the window-sill he had to let go of the pipe with his left hand. He inched along the ledge, clinging with his right finger-tips only, pressed flat against the wall, whilst below Tim bit hard on his thumb as he watched.

Gerry finally reached the window-ledge, weak and shaking with fright, his mouth dry and his throat so tight he could not call out to Tim who was dancing about and cheering.

There was a small space at the bottom edge of

the window and Gerry just managed to get his
fingers into it. Together he and the girl inside
heaved upwards, their faces flattened against the
glass.

The window suddenly slid up about a foot and Gerry cried out as he almost lost his balance. To make sure it did not happen again he sat down on the window-ledge, with his legs inside the room. Together they raised the window as high as it would go.

'Hello,' said Gerry.

'Hello,' replied the girl.

For a long moment they gazed at one another in an embarrassed silence.

'My name's Gerry, what's yours?'

'Anna,' replied the girl. 'I am Austrian.'

'What's going on here?' burst out Gerry in a rush. 'It's all shut up, yet you're living here – and who's that woman – oh, gosh – sorry, perhaps she's your mother?'

59

'No, no, no, she is not my mother,' cried Anna. 'She is supposed to look after me but she shuts me up here all day. She goes out all day and leaves me shut up here – I have not been out for nearly three weeks.' Anna was becoming more and more upset as she spoke, and finally burst into tears.

Gerry patted her on the shoulder, but could think of nothing to say.

Anna went on: 'We have just come to England, my father bought this house but before we could move in properly, he has to go back to Austria for Mother is ill. My brother Peter is there too. Frau Lindner was left to look after me – I wish my father was back,' and again Anna began to cry.

'Come on, Anna,' said Gerry. 'It's all right now, we'll get you out of here, and you can come and stay with us until your father comes back.'

'What's happening up there?' called Tim, jumping up and down with impatience.

Gerry went to the window. 'It's all right, Tim, we'll be down in a – oh! crumbs – the witch is back – quick, Tim. Hide!'

Gerry sprang back into the room, away from the window. Tim dived into the grass behind the tree and looked cautiously out to see if the witch had seen him. But she was still some way off.

'She hasn't seen me or she'd be shouting,' he called out in a loud whisper.

'Soon she will see the window open,' whispered Anna.

'Too late to close it now,' Gerry replied. 'What

can we do? We can't get down the tree in time.'

'We must stop the door,' said Anna, 'that will give us more time to make the escape.'

'Right,' said Gerry, 'but we must be quiet.' He picked up a chair, tip-toed over to the door and wedged it under the handle. Then they both silently lifted the table and stood it up against the chair.

'Anna! Anna!' came a shrill call from below.

'What shall I do?' whispered Anna nervously.

They looked anxiously at one another.

'Better see what she wants,' said Gerry. Anna went to the window.

'Yes, Frau Lindner?'

'Why is the window open?' she asked.

'I – I wanted to – some air – it is hot.'

'Close it at once!' shouted the woman; 'it is dangerous, you may fall.' Anna hesitated. 'Hurry, girl! Do as you're told.'

Reluctantly, Anna stood on a stool and reached up for the window.

'Say it's stuck,' hissed Gerry.

Anna pretended to pull a little more, then called:

'It's stuck, Frau Lindner.'

'All right, I'll do it when I come up. Wait.'

She hurried off round the corner whilst Tim flattened himself still lower in the grass.

'Quick now,' said Gerry, 'where are the beds?'

'Beds? In there,' said Anna, pointing. Gerry darted through the doorway, tore the clothes off the bed, dragged the sheets off and began knotting them together.

'Quick, Anna, get one off the other bed; three should do.'

Anna flung the covers off the other bed and dragged out a sheet. Gerry finished the first knot and began the second. As soon as it was done they rushed back into the other room.

'What can we tie it to?' cried Gerry despairingly. 'There's nothing.'

'Open the other window and tie it to the post,' said Anna.

Together they heaved at the other window.

'It won't budge,' gasped Gerry.

A key rattled in the lock of the landing door just behind them.

'She's there,' whispered Anna.

The woman shook the door and called, 'Anna! Anna! See to the door, it won't open.'

Anna called, 'Just a minute, Frau Lindner, I'm coming.'

Together they heaved again at the window.

'It won't move! It won't move!' gasped Gerry.

'Anna! Open this door at once!' Again the door shook on its hinges.

'Again,' said Anna. 'Heave!' cried Gerry, forgetting to be quiet.

Suddenly the window shot up and banged against the top.

'What is happening in there?' screamed the

witch woman. The door rattled furiously and the chair shook.

Gerry was swiftly knotting the sheet around the post between the windows.

'You can climb a rope?' asked Gerry anxiously. Anna nodded.

'Quick then, you first,' he said, as he finished the knot and tossed the end out of the window.

Anna jumped up onto the window ledge, seized the sheet rope and began sliding quickly down.

Gerry looked round anxiously at the bending chair as the door actually opened an inch or two. A furious eye glared in at him through the crack.

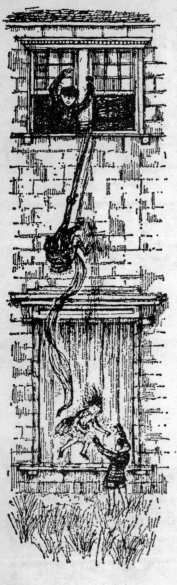

'You!' she screeched in a fury. 'What are you doing here?' She put her shoulder to the door and pushed hard. The chair began to skid along the floor and the table moved.

Gerry jumped up on to the sill and glanced down at Anna hanging on the end of the sheets.

'Drop, Anna! Drop! It won't hold two of us.'

Anna let go and Tim caught her as she landed.

Gerry began sliding down. Suddenly, the chair skidded away and the door burst open.

The witch rushed to the window but Gerry was already half-way down.

'You villains. I will call the police,' she screamed.

Gerry was on the lowest sheet when the knot

slipped. He spun dizzily as he fell and he felt as if his face hit the ground first.

'Gerry!' Tim cried, rushing up. 'Are you all right?'

The house was now spinning round above Gerry and the tree was whirling against the sky.

'Yes, I – I'm all right,' he said weakly, as the spinning went more slowly. Tim and Anna helped him to his feet.

'You have hit your lip,' said Anna, looking anxiously at Gerry.

'It's not much,' said Gerry. His head was no longer spinning, but his upper lip felt enormous.

'If you're feeling all right,' said Tim, 'we'd better run, the old witch

69

has gone in and she'll be down in a second.'

'Last one over the wall is a ninny,' mumbled Gerry through his swollen lip.

Together they ran for the trees.

7
The Telegram

They reached the wall and climbed safely down the ivy into the road without seeing the woman again.

'What are we going to do about it all now?' said Gerry, as they trudged home.

'I do not want to tell my father for he will worry,' said Anna.

'What exactly was she up to, the old witch woman?' asked Tim.

'Well,' said Anna, 'Father had given her enough money for two months in advance, but she is greedy and was going out to work all day as well. She was frightened to let me out even when she was there, in case I ran away or told the police.'

'Perhaps we ought to phone the police now,' said Gerry, who had always wanted to dial 999.

'Let's wait and see what your father says,' replied Tim. 'We'll come to your house first, Gerry.'

'All right,' said Gerry, looking wistfully across the road at the red telephone box.

'I suppose you used photographs to make the messages look genuine,' said Gerry.

'Yes,' replied Anna. 'I thought that if I used ordinary paper people would think it was a joke, or just children playing.'

'It was a jolly good idea,' said Tim. 'The boats, too.'

'You speak jolly good English,' said Tim.

'It's because my mother is Scottish,' said Anna laughing.

After another twenty minutes' walk they arrived at Gerry's house and had soon told Mr and Mrs Martin the whole story. Mrs Martin assured Anna she could stay as long as she liked.

'What about the police, Dad?' said Gerry, with one finger already in the dial of the telephone.

'No, Gerry, not yet,' said Mr Martin. 'I'd like

to see this woman myself first. I'll get the car out and we'll go now.'

'Wish we had a siren,' said Gerry, as they drove swiftly back. He imitated the sound with his hands cupped around his mouth making a deafening noise.

'Turn that thing off, Sergeant Martin,' said his father, laughing. 'I can hardly steer for the din.'

Mr Martin swung the car into the drive. There was a red flash as a motor cycle swerved out of the way and ran into the bushes.

'You all right?' asked Mr Martin, jumping out.

'Yes thanks, my fault, I was coming out the IN drive. Telegram for Frau Lindner, but no one's in.'

'It must be from Father,' cried Anna, joyfully.

'I suppose we'd better open it,' said Mr Martin, looking at the envelope. 'It may be urgent.' He handed it to Anna who tore it open, scanned it quickly, gave a whoop of joy and started dancing round and round the car.

'I gather he's coming soon,' said Mr Martin with a smile.

'Tomorrow!' sang Anna. 'Mother and Peter too!'

The telegraph boy grinned and roared off down the drive.

'What about the witch?' said Tim, when Anna had calmed down. 'Let's go to the house.'

'The telegraph boy said no one was in,' said Gerry, 'but she may not be answering the door.'

They ran to the house and found the front door open.

Together they went in, ran up the stairs and burst into the living-room.

The witch woman was standing in the middle of the room. She held a string bag in her hands and on the floor beside her was a battered suitcase. Her black clothes hung shapelessly on her like the bedraggled feathers of a wet bird. She suddenly seemed to have become much smaller. She had obviously been crying, and she twisted her damp handkerchief in her hands.

Tim noticed her hat for the first time, and now it seemed ridiculous, like the hat of a comedian. Gerry could hardly believe that this pathetic bundle was the witch who had frightened him so much.

She had been staring at the floor, but she looked up as Mr Martin followed them into the room.

'I saw you arrive,' she burst out in a rush. 'I

was about to go. I didn't mean to be unkind. I had
to have the extra money to send to my mother and
sister so that they can come to England too. I'll get
another job and pay it all back. I've put the rest
of the money on the table, and left my address
with it. I will stay with friends in the High Street.
If the police want me they will find me there.'

'We'll see what Anna's father has to say about that tomorrow,' said Mr Martin grimly, 'now you had better go.'

The old woman picked up the suitcase and shuffled out of the room.

'Poor old soul,' said Mr Martin, when she had gone. 'I think she was telling the truth, don't you?'

'Huh!' grunted Gerry, 'it's probably all an act. Let's get the police now.'

'No,' said Tim. 'I think she was genuine. I really began to feel sorry for her.'

'She didn't look very genuine to me,' said Gerry, though secretly he, too, had begun to feel sorry for the old woman.

'You don't look very genuine yourself,' laughed Mr Martin. 'But then, of course, you're not.'

Gerry grinned and aimed a playful punch at his father who ducked away as they all laughed.

'Now everything is wonderful,' said Anna smiling. 'Frau Lindner is gone and I am free and you must come here and we can have camps in the woods with Peter, and we can make fires and cook, and make huts in the trees. It will be wonderful.'

'Oh smashing. Thanks!' cried Gerry and Tim. 'We've rescued you for nothing now,' went on Tim smiling, 'now that your father is coming tomorrow anyway.'

'Not at all, not at all,' cried Anna, beaming. 'If you had not rescued me, I should not have found two such good friends for Peter and me. And what could be better than that?'

THE END

MIDNIGHT ADVENTURE

Written and illustrated by Raymond Briggs

Gerry and Tim are planning a midnight fishing expedition. All the details have been minutely worked out and the two boys can hardly wait to set off. But when they get to the lake on the golf course, it's not quite how they imagined. There are lots of creepy noises and they feel very alone.

Their suspicions are aroused when a lorry drives past them with its lights and engine switched off. It is heading for the golf club . . .

Gerry and Tim decide to investigate and there starts the adventure of a lifetime.

If you're an eager Beaver reader, perhaps you ought to try some more of our exciting titles. They are available in bookshops or they can be ordered directly from us. Just complete the form below and enclose the right amount of money and the books will be sent to you at home.

☐	HELLO MR TWIDDLE	Enid Blyton	85p
☐	THE ENCHANTED WOOD	Enid Blyton	95p
☐	THE MAGIC FARAWAY TREE	Enid Blyton	95p
☐	HEIDI'S SONG		95p
☐	URSULA BEAR	Sheila Lavelle	75p
☐	NICHOLAS ON HOLIDAY	Goscinny and Sempé	95p
☐	EMIL IN THE SOUP TUREEN	Astrid Lindgren	95p
☐	LOLLIPOP	Christine Nostlinger	£1.25
☐	THE WORST KIDS IN THE WORLD	Barbara Robinson	95p
☐	THE BROWNIES IN HOSPITAL	Pamela Sykes	95p
☐	THE GREAT ICE CREAM CRIME	Hazel Townson	85p
☐	THE MILL HOUSE CAT	Marjorie Ann Watts	£1.00
☐	BOGWOPPIT	Ursula Moray Williams	95p

And if you would like to hear more about Beaver Books, and find out all the latest news, don't forget the BEAVER BULLETIN. Just send a stamped, self-addressed envelope to Beaver Books, 17-21 Conway Street, London W1P 6JD.

If you would like to order books, please send this form, and the money due to:

HAMLYN PAPERBACK CASH SALES, PO BOX 11, FALMOUTH, CORNWALL TR10 9EN.

Send a cheque or postal order, and don't forget to include postage at the following rates: UK: 55p for first book, 22p for the second, 14p thereafter; BFPO and Eire: 55p for first book, 22p for the second, 14p per copy for next 7 books, 8p per book thereafter; Overseas £1.00 for first book, 25p thereafter.

NAME...

ADDRESS..

....

Please print clearly